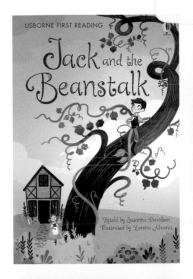

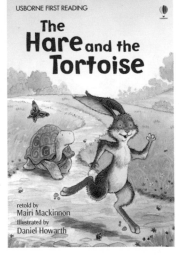

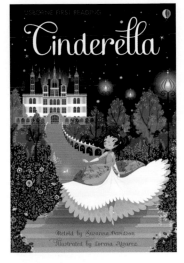

GOLDILOCKS
AND THE
THREE BEARS

Retold by Russell Punter

Illustrated by Lorena Alvarez

Reading consultant: Alison Kelly

Goldilocks lived with her father and mother near a forest.

She had curly golden hair and rosy cheeks.

Goldilocks looked like
a little angel...

but she was really a little
trouble maker.

She was naughty from morning...

to noon...

...to night.

And she never, ever did as
she was told.

One day, Goldilocks'
mother sent her to the village
for some bread.

"Do I have to go?" asked
Goldilocks.

"Yes," replied her mother, "and promise you'll go straight there and back."

Oh, all right!

Goldilocks hadn't gone far when she saw smoke.

"Where's that coming from?" she wondered.

Forgetting her promise,
she ran into the forest.

The smoke was rising from
the chimney of a pretty
thatched cottage.

Goldilocks skipped up to
the house and peered through
a window.

A wonderful smell
floated out.

Goldilocks pushed open the
front door and went inside.

She followed the smell to a large table, with three bowls of porridge.

So that's what it was.

Goldilocks' eyes lit up. "Lots of tasty porridge. Yummy!"

Goldilocks went straight for the biggest bowl. She stuck in a spoon and took a huge mouthful.

Instantly, her face turned bright red.

"Ouch!" cried Goldilocks, gasping for breath. "My tongue's on fire!"

15

"This middle size bowl looks cooler," thought Goldilocks.

She scooped up as much porridge as she could and gulped it down.

16

It was like swallowing
a snowball.

Too cold!

There was only one bowl left. "I hope it's better than the others," thought Goldilocks. She took a tiny taste...

...and, spoonful after spoonful, she ate up every last drop.

Goldilocks sighed. "All that eating has tired me out."

In front of the fireplace were
three chairs.

"That big one looks fun,"
thought Goldilocks.

She rushed up and threw
herself onto it.

"Ow!" cried Goldilocks.

Rubbing her sore bottom,
she moved to the next chair.

Goldilocks smiled. "That looks much more comfy."

She took a running jump onto the padded armchair.

"Ooof!" cried Goldilocks, sinking into the bulging cushions.

Finally, she tried the
smallest chair.

Until...

SNAP! The legs of the little chair broke clean off.

Goldilocks stared at what
was left.

She yawned. "What I really
need is a lie down."

Goldilocks climbed the stairs looking for somewhere to take a nap.

She soon came to a tidy
room with three beds.

Which one shall I choose?

There was a big bed,
a middle size bed and
a little bed.

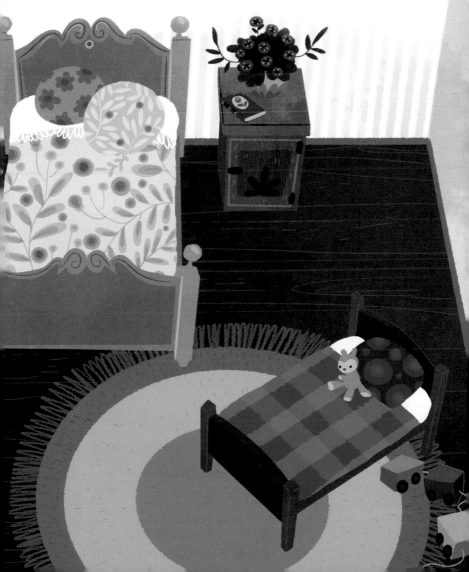

"That big bed has plenty of space to spread out," thought Goldilocks.

30

She clambered on top of the
huge mattress.

"This looks more like it,"
said Goldilocks, patting the
second bed.

"Help!" she called, sinking down. "I'm drowning in the mattress."

Too deep!

Finally, she came to the smallest bed. "I suppose this will have to do," she sighed.

Goldilocks sat on top. It was very, very comfortable.

She snuggled under the
covers. Moments later, she
was fast asleep.

Outside, the owners of the house returned from their morning walk.

"Who left the front door wide open?" asked Father Bear.

"It wasn't me," replied Mother Bear.

"Wasn't me," said Baby Bear.

Slowly, they crept inside.

"Someone's been eating my porridge," growled Father Bear.

"Someone's been eating *my* porridge," sighed Mother Bear.

38

"Someone's been eating *my* porridge," wailed Baby Bear, "and they've gobbled it all up!"

Then they saw the three
chairs by the fireplace.

"Someone's been sitting in my
chair," growled Father Bear.

"Someone's been sitting in *my* chair," sighed Mother Bear.

"Someone's been sitting in *my* chair," wailed Baby Bear, "and they've broken it!"

41

Just then, loud snores drifted downstairs. The three bears followed the sound...

"Someone's been sleeping in my bed," growled Father Bear.

"Someone's been sleeping in *my* bed," sighed Mother Bear.

"Someone's been sleeping in *my* bed," wailed Baby Bear, "and she's still there!"

Goldilocks woke with a
start. "Help!" she shouted

and she tore from the room.

Before the bears could say
a word, Goldilocks was outside.

Goldilocks ran and ran
until she reached home.

"I promise I'll do as I'm told from now on," panted Goldilocks.

"And I'll never, ever be naughty again," she added. And she never was...

...well, almost never.

About the story

Goldilocks and the Three Bears is an old fairy tale that has been told for many years. It first appeared in print in 1837 in a collection of stories by British author Robert Southey.

Series editor: Lesley Sims

First published in 2015 by Usborne Publishing Ltd., Usborne House, 83-85 Saffron Hill, London EC1N 8RT, England. www.usborne.com
Copyright © 2015 Usborne Publishing Ltd.

USBORNE FIRST READING
Level Four

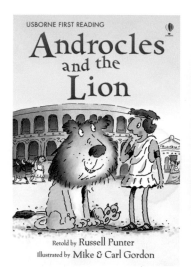

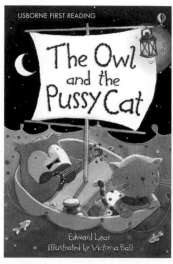

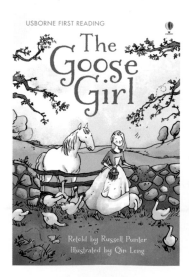

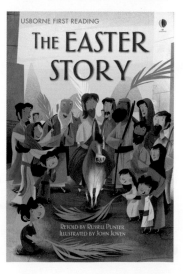